Brooke Boothby

A Letter to the Right Honourable Edmund Burke

Brooke Boothby

A Letter to the Right Honourable Edmund Burke

ISBN/EAN: 9783337192792

Printed in Europe, USA, Canada, Australia, Japan

Cover: Foto ©Andreas Hilbeck / pixelio.de

More available books at **www.hansebooks.com**

A

LETTER

TO

THE RIGHT HONOURABLE

EDMUND BURKE.

LONDON:

PRINTED FOR J. DEBRETT,

OPPOSITE BURLINGTON HOUSE, PICCADILLY.

M DCC.XCI.

A

L E T T E R, &c.

BELONGING to no party, addicted to no sect, and too old not rather to fear than to invite notoriety of any sort, may I not hope from among the few incitements which could induce such a man in love with retirement to obtrude himself on the public eye that I shall be allowed to assume the desire of being useful as my sole motive? " Conscious," to speak in the language of Lord Bacon, " that what I shall offer arises from no " vein of popularity, ostentation, desire " of novelty, partiality to either side, dis-

" position

" pofition to intermeddle, or any the like
" leaven ; I conceive hopes that what I
" want in depth of underftanding may be
" countervailed by fimplicity and fincerity
" of affection." Sure I am, Sir, that fuch
a difpofition will find favour in your fight;
that I fhall meet you ready to admit that
men may honeftly differ on topics where
the conclufions lie at fuch a diftance from
the premifes, and where the beft abilities
and the beft intentions fetting out from
the fame centre have been found to di-
varicate into every point of the compafs.

Permit me, Sir, before I proceed, to
offer you the humble tribute of my applaufe. I have for many years been
amongft the foremoft of your admirers.
I have feen you with uninterrupted energy
purfue the right, ftraight forward, and

fearlefs

fearlefs of confequences. I have feen you the foul of a great enterprize, which, though " offences' gilded hand may fhove " bye juſtice," or " the wicked prize itſelf " buy out the law," will fecure immortality to your name. When I differ from you in opinion, I am with you in fentiment. I regard you as one of the beft and ableft men of our day.

You have publiſhed a work abounding with eloquence, learning, knowledge, and every other excellence to be foretold of the production of a mind furniſhed like yours. But in the midſt of fuch good and found doctrine are maxims and pofitions which I think may be ufed by the worſt of men for the worſt of purpofes. The more you poffefs of thofe qualifications which give the opinion of one man authority over the rea-

fon

son of others, the more I feel it a duty, thinking as I do, to combat to the best of my power these dangerous tenets; to warn those who are about to feed upon your well-flavoured and high-seasoned dish that " there is death in the pot." Answerers you will have in plenty of various descriptions, with various motives, some of them most probably of much better abilities than I can pretend to; but I will cede to none of them in simplicity and purity of intention, or in respect for the person and character of the excellent man with whom I find myself so reluctantly obliged to differ.

To follow you, *non passibus æquis,* over the wide and flowery field where you disport yourself with so much dexterity and grace is by no means my intention.

I am

I am not one of thofe who, having taken a part, have an anfwer ready for every thing which can be offered on the other fide. In many things I agree with you moft heartily, and the high approbation I feel of much of your work gives me the more confidence where I am obliged to diffent. I have ftrong doubts, and offer them as fuch in fair difcuffion. I will endeavour to be as fhort as the time allotted me will allow of, for it belongs only to your pen to be diffufe without being tedious.

It is I think the peculiar infirmity of noble and ardent minds to run into extremes, to follow even the right too far. You are difgufted with the folly and danger of wild theories and extravagant projects, and would therefore reduce the
fcience

science of government to a mere craft and
myftery ; but politics muft have fome
abftract principles * Though flavery muft

* The moft meafured and technical writers have been
forced to confider natural liberty and the *rights of men* as
preceding all civil inftitutions. Sir William Blackftone,
who has never paffed for a light or factious writer, fpeaks
thus: " Thus much for the *declaration* of our rights and
" liberties. The rights themfelves, thus defined by thefe
" feveral ftatutes, confift in a number of private immuni-
" ties, which will appear from what has been premifed to
" be indeed no other than either that *refiduum* of *natural*
" *liberty* which is not required by the laws of fociety to
" be facrificed to public convenience, or elfe thofe civil
" privileges which fociety hath engaged to provide
" in lieu of the natural liberties fo given up by indivi-
" duals. Thefe therefore were formerly either by inhe-
" ritance or purchafe the *rights of all mankind*; but in
" moft other countries of the world, being now more or
" lefs debafed and deftroyed, they may at prefent be faid
" to remain in a peculiar and emphatical manner the
" rights of the people of England."
Montefquieu in his admirable Spirit of Laws treats
this fubject with his ufual neatnefs and perfpicuity:
" Les etres particuliers intelligens peuvent avoir des loix
qu'ils

be felt by the people, it may be foretold by the fage. To prophecy of fuch events, certainly much fagacity, and much experience, and much moderation are required, and many falfe prophets will arife who will deceive many ; but this is equally true in morality, religion, and every thing elfe that cannot be made the immediate object of demonftration ; and yet thefe are all reducible to fome great and general truths, which, when underftood, will be as univerfally affented to as that the three

"" qu'ils ont faites ; mais ils en ont auffi qu'ils n'ont pas
"" faites. Avant qu'il y eût des etres intelligens, ils
"" etoient poffibles ; ils avoient donc des rapports poffibles
"" et par confequens des lois poffibles. Avant qu'il y
"" eût des loix faites il y avoit des rapports de juftice
"" poffibles. Dire qu'il n'y a rien de jufte ni d'enjufte que
"" ce qu'ordonnent ou defendent les loix pofitives, c'eft
"" dire qu'avant qu'on eut tracé de circle tous les rayons
"" n'etoient pas egaux." Efp. des Lois, liv. i. chap. 1.

angles

angles of a triangle are equal to two right ones. The ſcience of politics may indeed be properly enough conſidered as a ſubdiviſion of moral philoſophy, capable of being treated ſynthetically with much advantage at this moment. What has happened in our own view in America, in Ireland, in France, are great and pregnant experiments. A treatiſe to which the proper title would be *The Philoſophy of Politics,* executed as I conceive it might be, would form an excellent and moſt uſeful work.

If the principles of the Revolution Club are as you tell us, but as I do not know that they acknowledge them to be, that the people of theſe realms are in a conſtant and habitual right and practice of * " chooſing

* Page 20.

" their

" their own governors"—" of cafhiering
" them for mifconduct"—" of framing
" a new government;" fuch folecifm
in reafon and fact feems fcarcely to deferve a ferious anfwer. The mifchief of
thefe doctrines, merges in their abfurdity. Is it not obvious to the flighteft
obfervation that before the people (who-
foever they are) can exercife the leaft of
thefe powers, all thofe of the actual conftitution muft be fufpended or done away,
a complete revolution muft have already
taken place? What do they mean by the
people? Where does this fourth eftate
exift? How is its collective voice to be
taken, or its collective force to act?
Where has it fo long lain perdue, and
from whence does it now come, like the
army in the Rehearfal, " to the door and

C   " in

" in difguife ?" When ftate quacks pre-
fcribe thefe recipes, I believe if they were
told, like their predeceffor in Moliere,
Why, Doctor, this is a Revolution, they
would anfwer as he does—a Revolution!
aye, Sir, and what is better than a Revolution! I ftrongly fufpect that all the fenfe
(if they have any) of thefe unintelligible
theories and vicious circles of the governed
governing the governors might be comprized in a plain propofition, to which I
for one would give my hearty affent;
that when government, under any form
or denomination offers oppreffion in the
room of protection, and injury inftead of
juftice; a ftone for bread and a ferpent
for a fifh, fuch government ought to be
refifted with all the powers which God
and nature have placed in our hands.

For

For this great and grievous difeafe, a revolution is the only true fpecific.

Since I have mentioned the Revolution
Club, I muft fay that I think you treat
Dr. Price's *nunc dimittis* * with very unde-
ferved afperity. If you think he errs, his
errour can only be fairly attributed to a
little too much ardour in a good caufe. All
enthufiafm is certainly excefs, it begins
where reafon ends; but an enthufiaftic
love of liberty has always been reckoned
amongft the moft ufeful and refpectable
infanities of the human mind. The Doctor
and many others with him will think, that
to hinder the King from erecting the royal
ftandard at Metz was of the laft import-
ance to the embryon liberties of France.
They will think that an immediate and

* Page 96.

moft

moſt probably a very blcody civil war was
cheaply prevénted by the exceſſes of the
mob at Verſailles on the 6th of October.
They will conſider the degradation of the
King with ſome ſort of complacency; not
as you ſay by reducing him to his qualities
of man or animal, for it is under theſe
titles only which he holds in common
with all of us that he can claim any pity
at all; but becauſe they ſee in his perſon the
actual living repreſentative of an oppreſſive
and intolerable deſpotiſm, the deſcendant
of old and the progenitor of future tyrants.
A pious divine, where he thinks he beholds
ſo much ſalvation, will very naturally break
out into thanks to God for what he believes to have been brought about by the
immediate interpoſition of his providence.
Grave and religious men and lovers of order

der too have burft into ejaculations on the recovery of liberty before Dr. Price. A great antient *ariftocrat*, whofe authority I believe you efteem more than I do, employs a ftill higher ftrain on a much more violent occafion. Speaking of the killing of Julius in the Capitol, he fays, What was there ever performed, O holy Jupiter! not only in this city but in the whole world greater, what more glorious, what more worthy of the eternal remembrance of mankind * !

For my own part, I cannot apprehend any fuch danger as you feem to fear from allowing men to fpeculate on the common-

* Quæ enim res unquam, proti fanctc Jupiter! non modo in hac urbe, fed in omnibus terris eft gefta major, quæ gloriofior, quæ commendatior hominum memoriæ fempiternæ! Cic.

· wealth

wealth as much as they pleafe. Speeches and fermons and pamphlets will produce but little effect, except where they find the minds of men predifpofed and ripe for the fubject. The bufinefs is already done before they can operate to any ftrong purpofe. They will only be ferioufly attended to when they give vent to fome paffion, or furnifh fome plaufible argument or excufe for what we are beforehand determined upon. While the people are happy and free they will no more be made to believe themfelves oppreffed and enflaved than all the oratory in the world will perfuade flaves and beggars that they are rich and content.

When you boaft to your French correfpondent, with fuch an air of triumphant confidence of the loyalty, the " religious
" zeal,

" zeal *," the obedience, the " fimplicity,
" the *bonhommie* of the Britifh † charac-
" ter," their " awe of Kings" and " reve-
" ence for [Priefts ‡," their " fullen re-
" fiftance of innovation ‖," their unalter-
able perfeverance in the " wifdom of pre-
" judice for the laft four hundred years §;"
are you not a little apprehenfive left he
fhould retort upon you the feven interrup-
tions of the hereditary fucceffion previous
to the Revolution; the public execution of
one King and the banifhment of another
a little before that period, and the priva-
tion and exile of a whole line of Kings immediately afterwards; four radical and en-
tire changes of religion in three fucceffive
reigns; Papift under Harry the firft de-
fender of the Romifh faith, and then Pro-

* Page 135. † P. 133. ‡ P. 128. ‖ P. 127. § P. 130.

teftant

teftant under the fame Harry the firft de-
fender of the Proteftant faith; violently
Papift again under his daughter the
Bloody Mary, and once more Proteftant
under her fifter Elizabeth; Prefbyterian under Oliver and the Commonwealth, An-
glican and Epifcopal at the Reftoration;
High Church under Anne, and Low Church
under the firft Georges; and at this very
moment feparated into as many fects as
there are fhades of opinion between the
wide extremes of bigotry and infidelity?

If a free and equal conftitution could have
been erected in France on the foundation of
the old eftablifhment, I am ready to allow
that to level all without diftinction was a
rafh and dangerous experiment. But this
does not appear to have been the cafe. A
century and half of defpotifm had fo warped
and

and moulded every inftitution to the fupport of the omnipotence of the Crown,
and to the annihilation of the liberty of the
fubject, that they could not be ufed for the
contrary purpofes. If the four eftates had
continued to meet in their antient form, the
nobles, the church, and the crown, pof-
feffing each of them powers utterly incon-
fiftent with a free conftitution, would have
united to render the reprefentatives of the
people, *le tiers etât*, a mere nullity. The
change from liberty to flavery may proceed by filent lapfe, but illegitimate force
muft be wrenched by violence from the
ftrong hand of power. The tyranny of
France could only be overturned by the
great mafs of the people. When this vaft
and unwieldy machine is once fet in mo-
tion, no mortal arm can exactly direct its

force,

force, or determine its momentum. We know that mankind in the aggregate muft be forced into activity by the immediate impulfe of fome ftrong paffion, and that their action will therefore always be accompanied with fome violence and fome excefs. We know too that change itfelf cannot be wrought without difturbance and diforder; the decompofition and combination of elements will be attended with commotion and effervefcence. But where much is to be obtained much may and ought to be hazarded: the utmoft that human prudence can provide againft future contingencies is to fecure the probabilities, the reft muft neceffarily be left to the great arbiters time and chance, to eventual courage and eventual ability. The deftruction of an inveterate tyranny, and

the

the probable eftablifhment of a free conftitution, muft be always confidered as cheaply purchafed at the expence of a few years
anarchy and diforder. In all ages thofe
citizens who fhall obtain for their country
fuch advantages at fuch a price, will continue to be ranked among the great bene-
factors of mankind.

The queftion then is reduced to this;
Whether the late government of France
was fuch as ought to have been endured.
It muft I think appear to every man who
acknowledges the ineftimable value of a
free conftitution that it was not. A government where the foundation of all law
is comprized in one fhort formula, FOR
SUCH IS OUR PLEASURE—CAR TEL EST
NOTRE PLAISIR; where the perfonal liberty, and confequently the property and

life

life of every individual, is held at the abfolute will and difpofal of one man; is a
government fhocking to the common fenfe
and common feelings of mankind. Neither the hereditary fucceffion of ages nor
the acquiefcence of millions can fanctify
abufe or change evil into good. Wrong
may be endured, but it cannot be eftablifhed. A bond in which no valuable confideration has been retained by one of the
contracting parties is void in law as well
as in equity. Poffeffion and prefcription
may be good titles *primâ facie*, but they
muft give .way when higher claims and
better rights are produced. I would confider it as a *datum* confirmed by the general fenfe and experience of mankind in
all ages, that an abfolute, or as you are
pleafed to call it, an unqualified monarchy

is

is no where to be fuffered. The prefervation of no order, no eftablifhment, can
compenfate for this enormous evil. Every
humane mind will anticipate with heartfelt fatisfaction the approach of that day
when the race of defpots fhall have difap-
peared from the face of the earth; and
when by their rufty coins and mutilated
ftatues they fhall be known to have ex-
ifted, it fhall be faid of them as of the
giants of old, " in thofe days there were
" tyrants in the land."

Will you permit me, Sir, to hazard a
conjecture? Twenty years ago you would
not have thought of this revolution as you
do now. In the fage caution I think may
be difcerned fomething of the timidity of
age; fome traces perhaps of the ftrong
impreffion made upon your vivid imagination

gination by the violences to which you
were an eye witnefs in the fummer of
1780. In your dread of diforder and mif-
rule you would counfel rather to bear the
ills we have of what magnitude foever,
quemvis durare laborem, than fly to others
that we know not of. " Your refolution
" is ficklied o'er with the pale caft of
" thought."

As the fource of the revolution in France
feems to have been purer, fo its procefs has
hitherto appeared milder than any in antient or modern ftory. The journal of the
fiege of Londonderry furnifhes more hor-
rours than all that we know of this great
event. A few obnoxious heads and fome
voluntary banifhments have been the only
facrifices to vengeance and the infernal
gods. Nor can thefe be fairly attributed
to

to any new fpirit infufed into the people by the diforder of the times. The execution of M. Foulon cannot be compared for atrocity with that of the Marechall D'Ancre, or the maffacre of the King's guards with the night of St. Bartholomew. And yet thefe happened before the baleful atmofphere of philofophy, the *azote* * in which no virtuous or falutary prejudice can continue to breathe, had poifoned the minds of men. When thofe very principles of loyalty and gallantry whofe fall you fo tenderly lament were yet in their meridian fplendour.

The humiliation of a King and the terrour of a Queen form under your pencil a very pathetic picture; a tragic and affecting leffon of the inftability of human

Page 132.

greatnefs.

greatnefs. You feem to confider thefe great perfonages, what in the day of their profperity they are always ready enough to confider themfelves, as above vulgar humanity. In their fufferings I fear they found that they were mere mortals. For my part, fo far from looking upon thofe who are born to crowns as being of a fuperior nature, I think they have not the common chance with the reft of mankind. It is out of our weakneffes and wants, the fweet intercourfe of fervices and benefits, that all the focial ties of charity and benevolence are formed. Men will feel for others what they apprehend for themfelves;

————Non ignara mali miferis fuccurere difco—

They will labour to obtain a fuperiour rank among their fellow mortals by fuperiority

riority in learning, or wifdom, or courage, or ufefulnefs, or virtue. But Kings as they are above the focial neceffities, fo they are above the focial feelings of life. Having no equal, they can have no friend nor no competitor; and ftanding on the pinnacle of greatnefs, to labour for any higher elevation by the common means of eminence muft appear to them like adding " another " hue unto the rainbow, or with taper- " light feeking the beauteous eye of hea- " ven to garnifh;—a wafteful and ri- " diculous excefs."——

As to the unhappy beauty whofe charms fo well deferve to be recorded in the fweet ftrain of your eloquence, I moft fincerely join with you in pitying her diftrefs becaufe I conceive it muft be very poignant. When you go forth the knight of this fair unfor-

tunate

tunate I shall be proud to be your squire.
In the mean time I do very truly hope
that together with the dignity of senti-
ment becoming her high birth and station
she also enjoys the heartfelt satisfaction to
reflect that she has not by her own conduct contributed to her own misfortunes;
that it is over her distresses only and not
over her faults that her friends and admirers would wish to draw a veil.

But let us turn from this sad lesson for
Kings, where we are constrained to pity
what we cannot much esteem, to the most
magnificent spectacle that has ever presented itself to the human eye. A great and
generous nation, animated with one soul,
rising up as one man to demand the resti-
tution of their natural rights. When it was
once determined that a free constitution

would

would be had, I have endeavoured to shew
by a short argument that the Nobles and
Clergy could not with any safety, be allowed to enter the fortress in embodied
strength. Their exclusive privileges and
oppressive territorial jurisdictions were
among the grievances most immediately
felt by the people. They presented an
eternal barrier to any substantial amend-
ment of the condition of the Commons.
It is to know little of the temper of
men born to high founding titles and lofty
pretensions, to suppose that these bodies,
possessing a commanding voice in the
legislature, would have made a voluntary
surrender of antient powers and splendid
distinctions derived to them through a
long succession of ancestry, merely because
these powers appeared incompatible with

E 2   a free

a free conftitution. They muft, on the common principles of prudence, habit, and inclination, have fided with the Crown againft the people. In this country it had been the policy of one of our antient tyrants, under their old maxim *divide & impera*, to ftrengthen the hands of the Commons by way of counter-balance, to the haughty and ungoverned claims of his feudal Barons *. From this

---

* By the ftatute *De donis*, eftates tail were rendered unalienable, and the large domains were of courfe fettled in perpetuity. By the decifion of the judges in *Talta-rum's cafe*, 12 Edw. IV. common recoveries were allowed to bar an eftate tail; and by the ftatute of 26 Hen. VIII. they were declared to be forfeited to the King in cafes of high treafon. By different ftatutes of Hen. VII. and Hen. VIII. a fine levied by a tenant in tail is al-lowed to be a complete bar to him and his heirs, and all other perfons. Sir William Blackftone obferves (2d Comm. 118), that it was the policy of Hen. VII. to lay the road as open as poffible to the alienation of landed property,

impure fource much good eventually
flowed, that was certainly neither intended
nor forefeen by the Monarch of that day.
The rank and title of nobility foon ceafed
to have any connection with territorial jurifdiction, and became attached
fimply to a legiflative and judicial peerage. Rich and powerful commoners and
a fubftantial independent yeomanry began
to form a real balance to the ariftocratic
part of the Conftitution; in procefs of
time it became the intereft of both to
unite, to circumfcribe the unbounded pretenfions of the Crown. In this country
every man who is not an actual member
of the Houfe of Peers is a Commoner.
Every Peer is born a Commoner, and

property, in order to weaken the overgrown power of
his nobles.

moft

moft of them have been at one time or
other members of the Houfe of Commons
in their own perfons; fo that they carry
up fomething of a popular fpirit into the
ariftocratical affembly. Many of the
leading men in the Lower Houfe look up
to the peerage either as their hereditary
right or as the ultimate reward of their
public fervices; an ariftocratic tendency
has therefore always prevailed among the
reprefentatives of the people. The fact is
that nothing of pure democracy or pure
monarchy, or pure ariftocracy, in a diftinct
or feparate ftate, is be found in our Conftitution. The three principles are blended and
tempered together into one common mafs.
They hold a joint undivided property. No
line of demarcation can poffibly be drawn
between them; nor can they ever be played

off

off againſt one another. This is one of the beautiful anomalies of the Engliſh government which diſdains all the fixed and known rules of political grammar. This is the *unity of intereſt* which is the foul of our great drama: the key-ſtone of the arch: the contripetal force that confines theſe eccentric bodies within their orbits. Hence the extreme inequality of repreſentation which ſounds ſo ill in theory almoſt diſappears in practice. The fabric exiſts in unimpaired beauty and ſtrength, not as is commonly ſuppoſed by preſerving the balance between contending and diſcordant principles, but by the firm uniſon and ſtrong texture of correſpondent and homogeneous parts. It may and probably will ſooner or later be ſapped by corruption, and its main timbers

confumed

confumed by the dry rot of influence;
but it has nothing to fear from wild theory
or treacherous ingenuity, from the cafhier-
ers of Kings or the afferters of paffive
obedience and divine hereditary right.

The government of France exhibited
the direct contrary of all this; an *unqualified* monarchy, a feudal nobility, a domi-
neering hierarchy, an impoverifhed and
fervile people. Divided intereft and dif-
jointed power. What was there here fo
well worth preferving? Were thefe the
corner ftones upon which you would have
laid the foundation of a free conftitution?
By what common ties of advantage, what
chain of gradual dependencies would you
have held thefe irreconcilable parts, thefe
jarring elements together? Till you have
fhewn what alchymy would have tranf-

muted

muted thefe bafe materials into filver and gold of ftandard currency, I muft for one continue to think that to amalgamate them into the common mafs, to refolve them into their natural individuality, and then to admit them to a fair and equal fhare in the benefits of a free conftitution was the beft that could be done. Perhaps in the event the noble families of France will not be found to have made fo bad an exchange. When the ftorm fubfides landed property and hereditary rank will flow back into their channels. Inftead of vaffalage to the Crown unworthy of a man to pay, and vaffalage from the people unworthy of a man to receive, thefe patricians will find themfelves among the leading reprefentatives of a free people, the legiflators of a great nation.

The abolition of hereditary titles of honour, which has been confidered as a mere wanton difplay of democratic envy or ill humour, had its peculiar neceffity in the peculiar conftitution of the body of nobility in France; differing *in toto* from any thing like what we know of here. That perfonal diftinctions fhould be hereditary at all is perhaps not very advantageous to public virtue any where; perhaps they ought to be referved as the perfonal rewards of public fervices; but however this may be, when they reprefent no refpectable public character like the judicial or legiflative peerage of thefe countries; when they ferve for nothing but to feparate the nation into the two foolifh and unnatural claffes of *gentil-homme* and *roturier* (a divifion which our language

language has not even terms to defcribe),
they are then not only barren of any good
but very mifchievoufly prolific in evil.
The refources of honeft induftry or inge-
nious invention were forbidden even to
the moft beggarly *hobereau,* fo that the
numerous poor nobility were really little
better than *ferfs* of the Crown, fhut up and
ranged in garrifons and citadels, always
ready to be employed againft the people;
while on the other hand the *roturier* by
no merit however great and ufeful could
ever be received into the other clafs. It
is not I think poffible to conceive a parti-
tion more unfavourable to liberty and all
virtuous exertion! In vain might you
have fought for a citizen in either of thefe
claffes; and the operation of this unhappy divifion accounts for that miferable

F 2   fpirit

ſpirit of uniformity and imitation ſo ſtriking in France to the ſlighteſt ob-ſerver. Much more *indeed* might be ſaid upon this ſubject which I muſt content myſelf thus barely to indicate.

How far the wiſdom and virtue of the leaders of the French revolution will be able to proceed towards forming the beſt poſſible government time alone can ſhew. All po-litical power conſiſts of an aggregate ſum of the natural rights and liberties of the per-ſons over whom it is exerciſed. In a juſt and equitable government no more liberty will be taken from the individual than is neceſſary to form an aggregate of power ſufficient to protect the whole againſt each, and each againſt the other. The beſt government therefore is that, under what denomination ſoever, where the

ſmalleſt

fmalleft quantity of liberty is exchanged for the greateft quantity of protection. Thefe legiflators are certainly called to a moft arduous tafk. They have not only the paffions and interefts of their adverfe parties but, what is much more dangerous, their own to contend with. Power is the ftrongeft of all tefts of human virtue, an ordeal almoft too fevere for the infirmity of our nature. During the formation of a new conftitution a dictatorial power muft however of neceffity be affumed by the lawgivers; and happily we are not without examples of fuch trufts faithfully exercifed for the purpofes of their inftitution, and then reftored into the hands of the people. Let us then hope for the beft. If avarice and ambition are ftrong motives, the love of glory

in

in generous minds is ftill ftronger; and
furely no fet of men in the annals of the
world had even a brighter profpect of being confecrated to the eternal admiration
and gratitude of pofterity than thefe men
have if they fhould complete what they
have fo glorioufly began.

But, alas ! with the Gothic feudalifm of
France, learning and the fine arts, and
honour and humanity have paffed away
from among men*; and Europe is on
the point of being once more overfha-
dowed with the darknefs of ignorance and
barbarity ! Men will become illiberal by
becoming free ! The liberty of the prefs
will put a final ftop to the diffufion of
knowledge ! Learning will not furvive
the lofs of its fyndics and licenfers, its im-

* Pag. 113, 114.

primateurs

primateurs, privileges, and approbations!
Honour muft perifh by extending its influence over a multitude of perfons hitherto
excluded from its jurifdiction! Humanity itfelf will be driven like another
Aftræa from the earth, by fubftitu ting the
foft gradations of unfelt dependencies to
thofe violent and hoftile diftinctions
which fever the commonwealth in twain;
where one half fears and hates, and the
other hates and defpifes! Farewel that
tender and ever wakeful providence of
government which fuffered no rafh
word or extravagant thought to efcape its
vigilance! That falutary coercion which
filently difpofed of a dangerous fubject
without fcandal or alarm! That beautiful inequality of conditions which, by
dividing men into diftinct and impaffible

orders

2

orders of beings, taught them to love as brethren! That convenient and levelling politenefs which makes vice amiable and virtue unneceffary! Farewel for ever thofe warm and foftering beams of arbitrary power alone favourable to genius and courage, to great conceptions and great atchievements! It was under your benign and genial influence, and not in the chilly atmofphere of a republic, that thofe miracles of valour and art were performed and produced which have ferved as models to all fucceeding ages, and which ftill continues to aftonifh the mind with the vaft fuperiority of their inimitable excellence! I confefs to you, Sir, the little knowledge and experience I have might have led me to conclude directly the contrary of all this. I fhould have

been

been apt too to think truth and fincerity and honefty and benevolence fufficiently lovely in the fimplicity of their nature without that prodigality of ornament and adfcititious decoration which you feem to confider as fo effential to them. Rich robes and coftly jewels I fhould have thought might be employed with advantage to conceal the uglinefs of the fmoaky image of Loretto, but could add no new grace to the Florentine Venus or the Roman Apollo.

In your view of France you feem to have been fo awe-ftruck with the magnificence of the court and fo enamoured of the rifing beauties of the Dauphinefs that you had no attention left to beftow upon the people. If at your return from Verfailles you had looked into the *Morne*,

where

where the bodies of thofe unfortunate wretches whofe miferies had drawn them· to feek the laft refuge from defpair were daily expofed in frightful numbers; if you had followed the peafant or the artifan to his fcanty meal on a morfel of black unfavoury bread, fuch fpectacles would not have been loft upon a heart like yours. They would furely have abated fomething of your partial regard for the deftructive fplendour of a court, or the redundant and invidious wealth of a lazy and luxurious priefthood.

Among the inftitutions to be fundamentally reformed or utterly done away before any fyftem of liberty could be eftablifhed in France the Papal hierarchy ftood prominent; and this is the inftitution whofe defalcation and reform you feem

moft

moft feelingly to deplore! To be called
upon in this country and at this day to
defend the Proteftant Reformation, the
leading motives of the Revolution in 1688,
the affociation of ideas fucked in with our
milk that Popery and flavery are as it were
convertable and fynonimous terms, feems
fo ftrange and extraordinary that all confideration of the fubject is at firft loft in
furprize. I believe however your paradoxes may be fafely entrufted to the ordinary fenfe of mankind notwithftanding
the authority of your name and the
fplendid oratory with which they are in-
troduced. It will not I think be neceffary on this occafion to difturb the repofe
of thofe controverfies by which the contrary principles were long ago eftablifhed.
When evident and practical truths have

G 2   been

been received into the mind fo as to form a kind of inftinctive fenfe, the diagrams by which they were at firft demonftrated, like the fcaffolding of a completed build-ing, may be fafely laid afide. Shall I now go about to prove by logical induction that liberty of confcience, not being in the *power* cannot be in the *right* of man to take away? or that belief not being fubject to human volition cannot be fub-ject to human controul? No, Sir, I will content myfelf with fimply recapitulating fome of thofe propofitions to which the minds of men in thefe countries have been fo long ufed to give fpontaneous affent, and then leave your paradoxes to fight their way through them as well as they can.

No

No man or body of men under any pre-
tence whatſoever can aſſume the power of
governing or forcing the belief, the
thoughts, the reaſon of others without
the moſt impious and fooliſh arrogance of
the power of God. Religion as a rule of
faith by which we are to be ſaved or con-
demned in another life muſt be the exclu-
ſive private concern of the individual, in
which every man has an indiſputable right
to follow the light of his own reaſon and
to reject all authority founded on the reaſon of others. Law is a rule of action only
and cannot be extended to the ſentiments
and feelings of men. Thoſe who denounce to us eternal damnation as the
conſequence of errour in faith, and then
would force us to hazard our immortal
ſouls upon their judgments who have no
concern

concern in the matter, contrary to our reafon who have fo deep an intereft in it, are the moft execrable of all tyrants. All temporal power in the Church is of mere human invention and amenable to human controul. Chrift has exprefsly declared that his kingdom is not of this world. If the Apoftles were obeyed it was from reverence of their virtues and not from any obligation; they received the voluntary gifts of the brethren, but they laid no claim to a tenth fhare in every man's poffeffions or the produce of his induftry. Excommunication was no more at firft, as the word imports, than expulfion from a club or fociety; and Bifhops only men of the wifer and difcreeter fort, chofen by the brotherhood to prefide over their ceremonies and to inftruct the ignorant, to

whom

whom all fubmiffion was entirely voluntary. In procefs of time this fociety became fufficiently ftrong to fet all civil go-
vernments at defiance; and then that fatal confederation between civil and ecclefiaftical power took place, under which
mankind has groaned for more than a
thoufand years. By this contract for the
bodies and fouls of men, the mind is firft
to be enflaved and then the body delivered
over to the fecular arm with its active
principle, the fpring of all its virtues and
faculties, bound up in chains. From this
complicated tyranny even death itfelf is
no refuge. Its power extends into the
kingdom of darknefs; the miferable mortal who has not obeyed its ordinances here,
who does not go to the grave clothed in
the *fan benito* of their inquifition and carry

in

in his hand the paffport of abfolution, is handed over to the agents of the hierarchy in another world ; to the difcipline of eternal torment.

Hierarchy confidered as a religious inftitution is contrary to the plain precepts of Chrift and to the whole tenor of the Chriftian religion. As a civil inftitution, where it has been moft modified and reformed, it is at beft an unneceffary burthen upon the induftry of the people and a dead weight in the preponderating fcale of power. In this country it is perhaps one of thofe evils fanctified by time which it may be more fafe to endure than to remove, but ftill calling loudly for reform. The ecclefiaftical courts are a crying oppreffion. The miferable and inadequate provifion made for the major part of the parochial.

parochial clergy is alfo a ferious grievance. In the place where I live the refpectable clergyman with a numerous family does the duty of a moft extenfive parifh for fixty pounds a year, while from the fame parifh the Dean of Lincoln receives a thoufand per annum for doing nothing at all *. The conftitution of the Papal

---

* One of the greateft and wifeft men this country ever produced ftrongly recommended it to reform thefe and other abufes 150 years ago. To thofe who affert it to be " againft good policy to innovate any thing in church" matters he fays ; " This objection is excellently anfwered " by the prophet ; ftand upon the *old ways* ; *and confider* " *which is the right or true way* and *walk therein.*" He " does not fay *ftand upon the old ways and walk therein :* " for with all wife and moderate perfons, cuftom and " ufage are indeed of reverence fufficient to caufe a " ftand, and to make them look about them, but no " warrant to guide and conduct them : fo as to be a juft " ground of deliberation but not of direction : and who " knows not that time is truly compared to a ftream " which carries down frefh and pure water into that dead " fea of corruption furrounding all human actions ?

H   Therefore

hierarchy in France bore a ſtrong analogy to that of her civil ſtate; it exhibited the two extremes without the intermediate parts. The prelates were rich luxurious lords and the country parſons rude and needy peaſants. And can you, Sir, ſeriouſly maintain that religion is likely to ſuffer by transferring its miniſtry from ſuch hands into thoſe of a ſober well regulated parochial clergy? The religion of Chriſt is peculiarly the religion of the

" Therefore if men ſhall not by their induſtry, virtue
" and policy, as it were, with the oar row againſt the
" ſtream and bent of time, all inſtitutions and ordi-
" nances, be they never ſo pure, will corrupt and dege-
" nerate. And I would aſk why the *civil ſtate* ſhould
" be purged and reſtored by good and wholeſome laws
" made every ſeſſion of parliament, deviſing remedies as
" faſt as time breeds miſchief, and yet the *ecclefiaſtical*
" *ſtate* continue upon the dregs of time and receive no
" alteration at all?" Lord Bacon's Philoſ. Works, 4to.
p. 308.

poor

poor and diſtreſſed ; his miſſion more eſpecially regards the meek and lowly. The
mild ſpirit of charity and love, the ſublime
and ſimple morality, the endearing and
conſolatory doctrines of the Goſpel will
not loſe their hold upon the hearts of
men, becauſe inſtead of Popes and Cardi-
nals and Archbiſhops and Deans and Ca-
nons they are delivered to them by plain
paſtors, their own choſen and immediate
guides. The power and authority of theſe
teachers will be preſerved by the ſame
means by which the voluntary ſubmiſſion
of free conſciences was at firſt obtained
by the apoſtles, " * by wiſdom, humi-
" lity, clearneſs of doctrine and ſincerity
" of converſation, and not by ſuppreſſion
" of the natural ſciences and of the mo-

* Hobbes.

H 2   " rality

" rality of natural reafon, nor by obfcure
" language, nor by arrogating to them-
" felves more knowledge than they can
" make appear, nor by pious frauds; nor
" by fuch other faults as in the paftors
" of God's church are not only faults but
" alfo fcandals, apt to make men ftumble
" one time or other upon the fuppreffion
" of their authority."

I will pafs over your apotheofis of
Monkery, and the neceffity for retaining
the Bifhops to take care of the confciences
of the Lords, for fear of being tempted
to more levity than is confiftent with refpect; however I will juft obferve that it
does not appear that there are any particular figns of reprobation among the
Nobility of Scotland who are deprived of
thefe fublime guides.

Men

Men have in different periods refifted fpiritual as well as civil tyranny in various degrees and with various fuccefs. The good fenfe and high fpirit of this country caft off the bonds of Rome at the firft dawn of reafon ;

——then might you fee
Cowls, hoods, and habits with their wearers toft
And fluttered into rags ; then reliques, beads,
Indulgences, difpenfes, pardons, bulls
The fport of winds.———

The political part of the Church govern-
ment has I fuppofe been wholly diffolved by the late reformation in France, and this was certainly the moft preffing object of a political revolution. The prefent mixture of religion with politics, our re-ligious tefts and parliamentary religion would I fufpect appear fomewhat ludi-

crous

crous to a perfon who could come to the confideration unbiaffed by habit and cuf-tom. Is it not a curious idea that if a Solon or a Socrates were to rife up amongft us one could not fit for Old Sarum, or the other execute the office of juftice of peace, Epaminondas could not command a troop of horfe or Themiftocles be made a poft captain, till they had made themfelves mafter of the Thirty-nine Articles previous to taking the facramental teft ? till they thoroughly underftood what Lord Bacon calls the characteriftics of a believing Chriftian * ?

---

* 2. He believes three to be one and one to be three; a father not to be older than his fon; a fon to be equal with his father; and one proceeding from both to be equal to both; as believing three perfons in one nature; and two natures in one perfon.

3. He believes a virgin to be the mother of a fon; and that very fon of hers to be her maker. He believes

How much of the trumpery of the
Church of Rome has been fuffered to remain I do not know nor is it I think of
much confequence. As foon as men are
allowed the free exercife of their reafon thefe wretched inventions of ignorance and folly will be prefently neglected
and forgotten. With the temporal power
the fpiritual jurifdiction, the vain and
fenfelefs theology of Rome will alfo pafs
away. The miferable diftinctions and fub-
tleties of the fchools, their abftract ef-
fences and fubftantial forms, their expla-
nation of the incomprehenfible myfteries
of religion by the incomprehenfible meta-

him to have been fhut up in a narrow cell, whom heaven
and earth could not contain. He believes him to have
been born in time, who was, and is from everlafting.
He believes him to have been a weak child, and carried in
arms, who is almighty; and him once to have died who
alone has life and immortality. Bac. Philof. Work, 4to.
Vol. XI. p. 235.

phyfics

phyſics of the peripatetics, will ceaſe to reſound from the benches of the Sorbonne and reſt for ever confined to the learned duſt of its libraries.

One of the moſt common objects of oratory is to perſuade men to believe ſomething more than we are willing to aſſert in plain terms or can prove by plain argument. I do not know that you any where ſay, in ſo many words, that all revolutions and reformations paſt preſent and to come are unlawful uſurpations, but I am ſure you labour hard to leave this impreſſion upon the mind of your readers. And what is ſomewhat curious in a whig by profeſſion you go over the ſame ground which the hiſtorians mention to have been taken by the tories in the Convention Parliament. In the looſe analogies

of

of declamation it is not difficult to confound revolution with rebellion, reformation with irreligion, refiftance with re-
volt, and a jealous love of the conftitution
with faction ; they have all fome features
in common, and by prefenting the refem-
blance and artfully concealing the difference might in the jumble be miftaken
for each other. But we will not be fo
deceived, we will diftinguifh between
them, nay more we will utterly deteft
and abominate the one and approve and
when neceffary vindicate the other, with
our lives and fortunes. In fupport of our
common fenfe and feelings we have the
higheft authority. The nation has fpoken.
.The decree is eternally recorded. " EN-
" DEAVOURING TO SUBVERT THE CON-
" STITUTION, BY BREAKING THE ORI-

I   " GINAL

" GINAL CONTRACT BETWEEN THE
" KING AND PEOPLE, AND VIOLATING
" THE FUNDAMENTAL LAWS," juftify,
nay fanctify refiftance and revolution.
This you are reluctantly and give me leave
to fay fomewhat awkwardly obliged to
admit, and the warmeft advocate for the
liberty of the fubject, the moft ardent lover
of the conftitution, can claim, can defire
no more. You fay, Sir, that you defire to
be thought no better a whig than Lord
Somers. Are you fure that you deferve to
be thought as good a one ? Let us com-
pare your whiggifm with his. You tell
us *, that " it is fo far from being true
" that we acquired a right by the Revo-
" lution to elect our kings (King Wil-
" liam the Third however was certainly

* Page 27.

2   elected)

" elected) that if we had poffeffed it be-
" fore, the Englifh nation did at that
" time (they chofe it muft be confeffed
" a very extraordinary moment) moft fo-
" lemnly renounce and abdicate it for
" themfelves and their pofterities for ever."
So then it feems the people *abdicated* as
well as the King! but before they could
abdicate the right they muft have been in
poffeffion of it. Now fetting afide the
confideration whether thefe men could
agree eventually to bind their pofterity in
chains which they themfelves were un-
able to bear, it muft be allowed that to
abdicate and renounce for their defcend-
ants for ever a right which they were at
that very moment afferting and actually
exercifing for themfelves, prefents a com-
plication of injuftice and abfurdity that we

ought

ought not to impute to our anceftors but upon the moft clear and fubftantial evidence that fuch was their intention. But you neither do nor can produce any fuch evidence at all. You reft your whole proof upon your conftruction of a refolution of the Convention Parliament which I will be bold to fay cannot poffibly be wrefted to any fuch conftruction in the judgment of any unprejudiced perfon who takes in the whole of the circumftances.

" The Lords Spiritual and Temporal and
" Commons do, in the name of all the
" people aforefaid, moft humbly and faith-
" fully fubmit themfelves their heirs and
" pofterities for ever (a common form of
" creating a fee fimple, which may never-
" thelefs be afterwards forfeited in various
" ways) and do faithfully promife that
" they

" they will ftand to, maintain, and defend
" their faid Majefties; and alfo the limit-
" ation of the Crown therein fpecified
" and maintained to the *utmoft of their*
" *power*" (remark by the way that thefe
laft are words of *limitation,* and not of *pur-*
chafe). Againft whom to defend them
in the name of common fenfe ? againft the
abdicated King, his fon, their defcend-
ants and adherents, and not againft any
future neceffity arifing from fimilar circumftances to thofe which were the very
origin, plea and foundation of this vote,
the corner-ftone of their whole proceeding!
And when they did interrupt the actual
fucceffion to eftablifh a new one, fo far
from binding themfelves as you feem to
infinuate to more general and unlimited
obedience, they actually contracted with
the

the Crown for the pofitive renunciation
of all its unconftitutional claims ; and they
fixed land-marks not only as due boun-
daries and limits to the Crown, but as no-
tices to the nation what the *conftitution* is
which they are not to fuffer *to be fubverted,*
what are the terms of *the original contract*
which they are not to fuffer *to be broken,*
and what their *fundamental laws* are which
they are not to fuffer *to be violated.* The
Declaration of Right is interwoven with
and actually forms part of the act which
fettles the fucceffion of the Crown. By
the Act of Settlement, upon which the
rights of the prefent Royal Family to the
Throne of thefe realms is founded, not only
a " temporary," but a perpetual " folution
" of continuity" took place. The hereditary fucceffion was intirely interrupted

in

in a whole male line, and William was *elected* King. Now Sir you muft either maintain that in interrupting the fucceffion and electing the Prince of Naffau the nation *ufurped* as well as *abdicated,* and fo vitiate the title of the prefent Royal Family, or you muft admit that the nation poffeffed the right which they then exercifed; and if you admit this, I defy you to fhew by any reafonable argument that we have not at this time exactly the fame rights which our forefathers had to do as they did in fimilar circumftances. If your mode of reafoning had been of any avail, there were not wanting men at that time to give it its due weight. Turner the deprived Bifhop of Ely among many others has taken from your pofitions all the graces of novelty, he has beat all the

ground

ground before you. He told the Convention Parliament that, " that being one " (fundamental) law which settles the suc- " ceffion, it is as much a part of the ori- " ginal compact as any; then if fuch a " cafe happens, as an abdication in a fuc- " ceffive kingdom, without doubt the " compact being made to the King, his " heirs and fucceffors, the difpofition of " the Crown cannot fall to us till all the " heirs do abdicate too. There are indeed " many examples and too many interrup- " tions in the lineal fucceffions of the " Crown of England: I think I can in- " ftance in all feven fince the Conqueft, " wherein the right heir hath been put " by: but that doth not follow that every " breach of the firft original contract gives " us power to difpofe of the lineal fuc-
" ceffion ;

" ceffion; efpecially, I think, fince the
" ftatutes of Queen Elizabeth and King
" James the Firft, that have eftablifhed
" the oath of allegiance to the King, his
" heirs and fucceffors, the law is ftronger
" againft fuch difpofition : I grant that
" from King William the Firft to Henry
" the Eighth there have been feven inter-
" ruptions of the legal line of hereditary
" fucceffion ; but I fay, thefe ftatutes are
" made fince that time, and the making
" of new laws, being as much a part of
" the original compact as the obferving
" of old ones, or any thing elfe, we are
" obliged to purfue thofe laws, till altered
" by the legiflative power, which fingle
" or jointly, without the Royal affent, I
" fuppofe we do not pretend to"—" I hope
" and am perfuaded, that both Lords and

K   " Com-

" Commons do agree in this, not to *break*
" *the line of fucceffion* fo as make the Crown
" *eleɛtive.*"

Now hear Lord Somers—" The word
" abdicate, doth naturally and properly
" fignify entirely to renounce, throw off,
" difown, relinquifh any thing or perfon
" fo as to have no further to do with it;
" and that whether it be done by exprefs
" words, or by doing fuch *aɛts as are in-*
" *confiftent with the holding or retaining*
" *of the thing.*" " That King James the
" Second hath renounced to be a King
" according to the conftitution, by avowing
" to govern by a defpotic power unknown
" to the conftitution, and confiftent with
" it he hath renounced to be King *ac-*
" *cording to the law.* Such a King as he
" fwore to be at the coronation, fuch a
" King

" King to whom the allegiance of an
" Englifh fubject is due, and hath fet
" up another kind of dominion, which is
" to all intents and purpofes an abdica-
" tion or abandoning of his legal title,
" as fully as if it had been done by exprefs
" words."

Hear too Lord Chief Juftice Holt—
My Lords, " Both in the common law of
" England, and in the civil law, and
" in common underftanding, there are
" exprefs acts of renunciation that are
" not by deed; for if your Lordfhips
" will pleafe to obferve the *government*
" *and magiftracy is under a truft*, and any
" *acting contrary to that truft is renoun-*
" *cing of the truft* though it be not a re-
" nouncing by formal deed; for it is a
" plain declaration by act and deed,

K 2 " though

" though not in writing, that he *who hath*

"_ *the truſt*, acting contrary, is a declaimer

" of the truſt ; eſpecially, my Lords, if

" the actings be ſuch as are *inconſiſtent*

" *with, and ſubverſive of the truſts*; for

" how can a man in reaſon or ſenſe, ex-

" preſs a greater renunciation of a truſt,

" than by the conſtant declarations of

" his actions to be quite contrary to that

" truſt ?"

Now Sir whether your whiggiſm moſt reſembles that of Lord Chancellor Somers and Chief Juſtice Holt or that of the non-juring ex-biſhops I will leave to your own candour to decide.

You give your French correſpondent to underſtand that a vaſt majority of " not " the leaſt learned and reflecting men of " this kingdom" totally diſapprove and abhor

abhor the whole foundation and proceedings of the Revolution in France. In
the retirement in which I live, I have the
good fortune fometimes to converfe with
perfons deferving at leaft of this defcription (for they are not all confined to courts
and capitals) and the refult of my obfervation has been very different indeed from
that of yours. Thefe perfons have appeared to me to confider the grounds and
motives of this Revolution as perfectly
legitimate. To have tried it upon the
principles of our own revered Revolution,
and to have found in their verdict that the
conftitution of France *had been long fubverted, the original contract between King
and People long broken,* and the *fundamental laws long violated.* Far from confi-
dering the nafcent liberties of France

with

with envy or averfion they have feemed
to look forward with a warm and lively
hope to the final eftablifhment of civil
and religious freedom in that great nation ;
perhaps to have extended their views into
the beautiful perfpective of general liberty
and general toleration. Upon the wifdom or expediency of the acts of the Na-
tonal Affembly they have not indeed
appeared fo ready to decide, they have
thought it more decent and refpectful to
fufpend their judgment till the final hear-
ing of the caufe, to leave to the perfons
immediately concerned the management
of their own affairs, and the confideration
of their own interefts, and not to give
extrajudicial opinions *pendente lite* in a
fuit in which they are neither plaintiff
nor defendant nor advocate nor judge.

If

(71)

If you Sir have thought this prudent caution unneceſſary, I am perſuaded you
have been provoked to think ſo by certain
indiſcreet applications made or ſuppoſed
to be made of what is now doing in France
to what might or ought to be done here.
The extreme ardour of your zeal cannot
eaſily be otherways underſtood.

You give as Rouſſeau's a ſecret for ex-
citing the callous attention of the public
which might otherwiſe perhaps have been
ſuſpected to be a receipt of your own *. It
has been ſaid of him that his deductions are
logical and exact from premiſes which are
ſometimes falſe. In this indeed you differ, for your firſt poſitions may for the
moſt part be ſafely admitted and your con-
cluſions ſhould I think be very frequently

Page 251.

rejected.

rejected. And yet I believe the errours as well as the beauties of the writings of both derive much from the fame fource, a too exquifite even to a morbid feeling of your fubject. Rouffeau was a man of great fincerity and far above any fuch little art as you fay Hume attributed to him; fo, Sir, are you; but you have un-governed imaginations. The modefty of reafon is dazzled and confounded amid the brilliant blaze of your imagery and invention. You are driven out of your courfe by crowding too much fail in pro-portion to your ballaft. In fuch lan-guage as yours a man may (to borrow a French term) *dereafon* with a great deal of eclat and fuccefs; plain matter-of-fact writers might often anfwer you fufficiently by tranflating your eloquent periods, where

" imagi-

" imagination bodies forth the forms of
" things unknown"—into common language, the vulgar idiom.

Becaufe the tenets attributed to certain
focieties feem to ftimulate to premature or
unneceffary refiftance you attack all reform. You fee a machine leaning to one
fide and you redrefs it with fo much redundant ftrength towards the other, that
inftead of reftoring it to its true perpen-
dicular medium, you force it into a more
violent and I think a much more dangerous inclination ; for if we were to admit
one of the extremes, either that the nation may at any moment cafhier one King
and elect another ; or that in no cafe
whatfoever the nation can interrupt or
change the hereditary fucceffion of the
Crown, I muft confider the firft alterna-

L   tive

tive as the foundeft in principle and the
fafeft in practice; for after all modify it
how you will, in fpite of all the addrefs
with which you endeavour to keep the
" fmall and temporary folution of con-
" tinuity from the eye*," your diminutive
epithets qualifying phrafes and " pious
" legiflative ejaculations," in fpite of the
pains you take to " countenance and fofter
" and make the moft of the idea of an
" hereditary fucceffion," in fpite of your
attempt to confound *expediency* with *ne-*
ceffity †, it will at laft remain an undeniable
fact that James was " cafhiered" and that
William was " elected."

 " How," you afk ‡, " does the fettle-
" ment of the Crown in the Brunfwick
" line come to legalize our monarchy

  * Page 24.   † P. 23.   ‡ P. 19.

          " rather

" rather than that of any of the neigh-
" bouring countries ?" For this plain reafon, becaufe the Houfe of Brunfwick was
called to the throne by the national choice
in preference to the Houfes of Stuart and
Savoy and Bourbon, as more likely to preferve and maintain our civil and religious
rights ; and becaufe the Houfe of Brunfwick accepted of the Crown under con-
tracts and ftipulations known, ratified and
recorded; nothing like which has ever
happened that I know of in any neigh-
bouring monarchy.

You tell us too that the ftatute *De
tallagio non concedendo* *, the *Petition of
right*—the act of *Habeas Corpus* depend
upon the validity of the title of the King
by whom they were affented to ; but this

* Page 31.

L 2   I utterly

I utterly deny. The privileges ratified
by thefe acts were not in the gift of any
King; they were " the true antient and
" indubitable rights of the people of this
" kingdom †."

If, Sir, you had confined yourfelf to
expofing the hollow and fhapelefs phan-
toms exifting, if they exift at all in the
brains of a few fenfelefs enthufiafts,

—The brood of folly without father bred—

and to the examination of the wifdom and
equity of the proceedings of the National
Affembly, you would never have been
troubled with any obfervations of mine.
But you have gone much and I think
moft unneceffarily farther: you have attacked the fundamental principles of all
reform: you have brought the fubject

* Bill of Rights.

which

which appeared at such a distance home to our own bosoms—*tua res agitur*—you have revived old disputes and subsided heats, evoked the sleeping shades of Jacobites and Republicans, and called up into untimely resurrection the long forgotten animosities of Roundhead and Cavalier. You have made it necessary for us *now* to examine when and how, under what pressure of evil and under what sanction of right, a revolution may ever again at any future period be recurred to in this country.

It is of the essence of power to encrease by its own force; wherever the greatest quantum is found, to that all inferior quantities will gravitate as to a common centre. For this reason Mr. Locke when he gave a form of government to one of the Co-

lonies

lonies in America limited its duration to an hundred years. To fabricate eternal machinery either phyfical or moral belongs only to the hand of God. Nay fo far has God himfelf condefcended to the verfatility of his creatures that he has already given us two difpenfations differing confiderably from each other. The very regulation of time by which every thing elfe is regulated has been found fubject to errour and requiring change. To the Julian has fucceeded the Gregorian fyftem, and to that another muft fucceed if the world fhould fo long endure. Our poor little inftitutions like our watches require to be periodically wound up and frequently repaired. They all contain in their very effence and original concoction latent principles of deftruction. It is the

beft

beſt office of the collective wiſdom of the times to mark the decay and to retard its progreſs, and when the day comes, as come it muſt ſooner or later, that the machine ceaſes entirely to anſwer the purpoſes for which it was conſtructed, to direct the formation of a new one if poſſible on a better principle and of more durable materials.

In this country thoſe who conſider the immenſe and growing influence of the Crown in addition to powers which had been already deemed ſufficient for its ſupport, will not I think be at a loſs to prognoſticate the malady which will one day give the mortal blow to our boaſted conſtitution. Corrupt influence is its radical diſeaſe, it will encreaſe with our riches and peace and proſperity;

The

The young difeafe that muft fubdue at length
Grows with our growth and ftrengthens with our
ftrength.

This polypus in the heart of the conftitution will carry it off by a fudden
blow full of life and vigour, and without
much warning. The conqueft of America by the King's troops, would moft
probably have greatly accelerated this
event; as the increafe of Indian gold and
Indian influence now bid fair to haften its
approach.

By way of deterring us in this country
from meddling in the myfteries of ftate,
and to " operate with a wholefome awe
" upon free citizens," you tell your correfpondent that our commonwealth is
" *confecrated**," that its " very defects and

Page 143.

" corrup-

" corruptions are to be approached"
" with pious awe and trembling folici-
" tude." You denounce the fate of
Uzzah, whom God fmote for his errour,
" becaufe he put forth his hand and took
hold of the ark of God when the *oxen*
fhook it, on all thofe who fhall dare to examine with facrilegious curiofity this my-
ftical hypoftatic union of Church and State.

With a little lefs of the terrible and
fomewhat more of *enjouement*, you in another place advife us to leave altercation
and take to enjoyment.

Ut melius, quidquid erit, natis !

And then again you quit this epicurean
indifference for quite another ftrain *, and
allow that a " jealous ever-waking vi-

* Pag. 79;

M   " gilance

" gilance to guard the treasure of our
" liberty, not only from invasion but
" from decay and corruption is our best
" wisdom and our first duty."

· What an admirable writer has said in answer to the preachers up of all this effeminate timidity in probing the wounds of the state; what he urges with irresistible force on those who would persuade us that at the time we guarded ourselves from one mode of oppression we covenanted to submit to every other, is so strong in point, replete with so much intelligence and intimate knowledge of the subject, so apposite to the present times, and so deserving of constant attention, that I will indulge myself in the liberty of making a very long quotation. To what in substance I might have said myself, I will superadd

the

the authority of a great name, and the
energy of moſt eloquent language *. " It
" is not to be argued †," ſays this great
orator, " that we endure no grievances be-
" caufe our grievances are not of the ſame
" ſort with thoſe under which we labour-
" ed formerly; not precifely thoſe which
" we bore under the Tudors, or vindicated
" on the Stuarts. " ‡ No complaiſance
" to our Court, or to our age, can make
" me believe nature to be ſo changed, but
" that public liberty will be among us,
" as among our anceſtors, obnoxious to
" ſome perſon or other ; and that oppor-
" tunities will be furniſhed for attempting
" at leaſt ſome alteration to the prejudice
" of our conſtitution. Theſe attempts

* Thoughts on the Cauſe of the preſent Diſcontents.
† Page 8. ‡ Page 10.

" will

" will naturally vary in their mode, ac-
" cording to times and circumſtances; for
" ambition, though it has ever the ſame
" general views, has not at all times the
" ſame means, nor the ſame particular
" objects. A great deal of the furniture
" of antient tyranny is worn to rags, and
" the reſt is entirely out of faſhion. Be-
" ſides there are few ſtateſmen ſo very
" clumſy and awkward in their buſineſs,
" as to fall into the identical ſnare which
" has proved fatal to their predeceſſors.
" When an arbitrary impoſition is at-
" tempted upon the ſubject, undoubtedly
" it will not bear on its forehead the name
" of *ſhip-money*. There is no danger that
" an extenſion of the *foreſt-laws* ſhould be
" the choſen mode of oppreſſion in this
" age ; and when we hear any inſtance of
                                    " mi-

" minifterial rapacity to the prejudice of
" the rights of private life, it will cer-
" tainly not be the exaction of two hun-
" dred pullets from a woman of fashion for
" leave to lie with her own hufband.
" Every age has its own manners and its
" politics dependant upon them, and the
" fame attempts will not be made againft
" a conftitution fully formed and matured
" that were ufed to deftroy it in the cra-
" dle, or to refift its growth during its
" infancy.

    " Againft the being of Parliament I am
" fatisfied no defigns have ever been enter-
" tained fince the Revolution. Every one
" muft perceive that it is ftrongly the in-
" tereft of the Court to have fome fecond
" caufe interpofed between the Minifter
" and the people. The gentlemen of the
                                    " Houfe

" Houfe of Commons have an intereft
" equally ftrong in fuftaining the part of
" that intermediate caufe. However they
" may hire out the *ufufruct* of their
" voices, they never will part with the
" *fee and inheritance*. Accordingly thofe
" who have been of the moft known de-
" votion to the will and pleafure of a
" Court have at the fame time been
" moft forward in afferting an high autho-
" rity in the Houfe of Commons. When
" they knew who were to ufe that au-
" thority and how it was to be employ-
" ed, they thought it could never be car-
" ried too far. It muft be always the
" wifh of an unconftitutional ftatefman,
" that an Houfe of Commons who are
" entirely dependant upon him, fhould
" have every right of the people entirely
                                    " de-

" dependant upon their pleafure. It was
" foon difcovered that the forms of a
" free and the ends of an arbitrary govern-
" ment, were things not altogether in-
" compatible.

" The power of the Crown, almoft
" dead and rotten as prerogative has grown
" up anew with more ftrength and far lefs
" odium, under the name of influence ;
" an influence which operated without
" noife and without violence ; an influence
" which converted the very antagonift
" into the inftrument of power; which
" contained in itfelf a perpetual principle
" of growth and renovation ; and which
" the diftreffes and the profperity of the
" country equally tended to augment, was
" an admirable fubftitute for a preroga-
" tive, that being only the offspring of
                                    " anti-

" antiquated prejudices, had moulded in
" its original ftamina, irrefiftible prin-
" ciples of decay and diffolution. The
" ignorance of the people is a bottom but
" for a temporary fyftem ; the intereft of
" active men in the ftate is a foundation
" perpetual and infallible.

" * They who will not conform their
" conduct to the public good and cannot
" fupport it by the prerogative of the
" Crown have adopted a new plan. They
" have totally abandoned the fhattered and
" old-fafhioned fortrefs of prerogative, and
" made a lodgment in the ftrong hold of
" Parliament itfelf.

" If they have any evil defign to which
" there is no ordinary legal power com-
" menfurate, they bring it into Parlia-

* Page 70.

" ment.

" ment.   In Parliament the whole is ex-
" ecuted from the beginning to the end;
" in Parliament the power of obtaining
" their object is abfolute and the fafety
" in the proceeding perfect. No rules
" to confine, no after-reckonings to ter-
" rify. Parliament cannot with any great
" propriety punifh others for things in
" which they themfelves have been ac-
" complices. Thus the controul of Par-
" liament upon the executory power is
" loft, becaufe Parliament is made to par-
" take in every confiderable act of go-
" vernment.

" * I muft beg leave †, ' however,' to
" obferve, that no part of the legiflative
" rights can be exercifed without regard
" to the general opinion of thofe who are

----

* Letter to John Farr and John Harris.   † Page 50.

N   " to

" to be governed. That general opinion
" is the vehicle and organ of legiflative
" omnipotence; without this it may be
" a theory to entertain the mind, but it is
" nothing in the direction of affairs. The
" completenefs of the legiflative authority
" of Parliament over this kingdom is not
" queftioned; and yet many things indu-
" bitably included in the abftract idea of
" that power, and which carry no abfo-
" lute injuftice in themfelves, yet being
" contrary to the opinion and feelings of
" the people, can as little be exercifed as
" if the Parliament in that cafe had been
" poffeffed of no right at all. I fee no
" abftract reafon which can be given why
" the fame power which made and re-
" pealed the High Commiffion-Court and
" the Star Chamber might not revive
                                   " them

" them again ; and thefe courts, warned
" by their former fate, might poffibly
" execute their power with fome fort of
" juftice. But the madnefs would be as
" unqueftionable as the competence of that
" Parliament which fhould attempt fuch
" things *. In effect to follow not to
" force the public inclination, to give a
" direction, a form, a technical drefs, and
" a fpecific fanction to the general fenfe
" of the community, is the true end of
" legiflature. It is fo with regard to the
" exercife of all the powers which our
" conftitution knows in any of its parts,
" and indeed to the fubftantial exiftence
" of any of the parts themfelves.

" + If there be one fact in the world
" perfectly clear it is this; that the dif-

* Page 52. + P. 55.

N 2 " pofition

" pofition of the people of *thefe countries* *

" is wholly averfe to any other than a free

" government. If any afks me what a

" free government is, I anfwer, that for

" any practical purpofe it is what the

" people think fo ; and that they, and not

" I, are the natural, lawful, and compe-

" tent judges of this matter.

" Liberty" ' muft indeed' † be limited

" in order to be poffeffed ‡ ; but liberty

" is a good to be improved, not an evil

" to be leffened. It is not only a private

" bleffing of the firft order, but the vital

" fpring and energy of the ftate itfelf,

" which has juft fo much life and vigour

" as there is liberty in it. But whether

" liberty be advantageous or not (for I

" know it is a fafhion to decry the very

* America in the original.   † Page 57.   ‡ P. 58.

" prin-

" principle) none will difpute that peace
" is a bleffing; and peace muft in the
" courfe of human affairs be frequently
" bought by fome indulgence and tole-
" ration at leaft to liberty. For as the
" Sabbath (though of Divine inftitution)
" was made for man, not man for the
" Sabbath, government, which can claim
" no higher origin or authority, in its ex-
" ercife at leaft, ought to conform to the
" exigencies of the time and the temper
" and character of the people with whom
" it is concerned; and not always to at-
" tempt violently to bend the people to
" their theories of fubjection. The bulk
" of mankind on their part are not ex-
" ceffively curious concerning any the-
" ories whilft they are really happy; and
" one fure fymptom of an ill-conducted
" ftate

" ftate is the propenfity of the people to
" refort to them.

   " But when fubjects by a long courfe
" of ill conduct * are once thoroughly in-
" flamed and the ftate itfelf violently dif-
" tempered, the people muft have fome
" fatisfaction to their feelings more folid
" than a fophiftical fpeculation on law and
" government †.—*General* rebellions and
" revolts of a whole people never were
" *encouraged*, they are always *provoked*.—
" Can it be true loyalty to any govern-
" ment ‡ or true patriotifm towards any
" country to flatter their pride and paf-
" fions rather than to enlighten their
" reafon ?"

This fame great author (for I love to
avail myfelf of his name and abilities) for-

* Page 59.   † P. 4.   ‡ P. 42.

merly

merly expofed by arguments to which time and experience have fince fet their feal, the danger of the policy adopted in the beginning of the prefent reign, of breaking up the great parties into which the nation had been divided from the time of the Revolution *. Thefe parties certainly formed a barrier between the people and the Crown. They embodied as it were Adminiftration. They entered into a recognizance with the public for Minifters and gave a broader furface to refponfibility. They ferved too as a mutual counterpoife and check upon one another; and each in turn became bound by intereft, the ftrongeft tie, to make common caufe with the people. Each had a reputation to preferve and each acted under the pene-

* Thoughts on the Caufe of the prefent Difcontents.

trating

trating and fufpicious eye of a rival. By their conftant ftruggles for popularity, then neceffary to any permanency in power, the flame of liberty was ventilated and kept alive. Public opinion while it fat as um-pire between the pretenfions of thefe great contending parties preferved its due weight and confequence in all public affairs.

A great part of this has been fince done away and we may deprecate the hour when the work fhall be completed. If we fhould ever fee a Minifter ftanding firmly on the ruins of all parties, uncon-nected and alone, filling the Houfe of Lords with unknown and unconnected men, and every office of the ftate with young re-cruits to be drilled in his own difcipline againft future contingencies, keeping all

the

the wifdom and virtue and ability and confequence of the nation at a diftance, that
he himfelf may be the only figure among
cyphers, captivating the vulgar by fmall
temporary arts, and lavifhing with unbounded prodigality the immenfe patron-
age of the Crown to procure an unheard-
of allegiance to his perfon and a blind and
abject fubmiffion to his will in the two
Houfes of Parliament; 'fuch a Minifter
would prefently be found to have no other
boundary to his power than the extent of
his ambition. He might pull off the
mafk when he pleafed. The confidence
and good opinion of the nation might or
might not be the object of his tafte, but
it muft very foon ceafe to be neceffary for
his protection. Under fuch a Minifter we
might perhaps maintain our confequence

O   among

among foreign nations, and our wealth and commerce might flourifh and encreafe: all this happened to France under Richlieu; but our liberties and laws would ftand upon a moft hollow and unfafe foundation. The *government* might be ftrong and powerful, but the *conftitution* would foon find itfelf attacked with a moft dangerous, perhaps fatal paralyfis.

Let us for the fake of argument fuppofe ourfelves, what I fhould conceive the ken of your mental eye would find no very difficult vifion, carried forward into a period of time, I hope a diftant one, when the ftagnant and ftinking waters of corruption fhall have pervaded every avenue of the State; when there fhall be a Houfe of Commons chiefly confifting of placemen, penfioners, hungry expec-
tants,

tants, India delinquents, and every other defcription of Minifterial dependants, kennelled like hounds and crouching for employment; reprefentatives reprefenting nothing but their own perfonal interefts; a Houfe of Lords of new creatures of the Minifter and old valets of the King, courtly lawyers and a courtly hierarchy—Nihil ufquam prifci aut integri moris; omnes, exutâ æqualitate, juffa principis afpectantis; the nation itfelf infected with a narrow felfifh egotifm, where every man feels himfelf the central point of his own little circle of luxuries and conveniences, and holds a ftupid indifference to the public concern. I have ftated, I think, nothing impoffible to conceive, or unlikely to happen from our actual tendencies; under fuch a fuppofition, even you, Sir, will I believe

allow,

allow, that though the forms of the conftitution might be preferved and the laws
yet remain inviolate, all the liberty the
people were ftill permitted to enjoy might
be fairly confidered as held at the will of
the Crown ; it would ftand upon no
deeper a foundation than the perfonal
virtue of the Brunfwick of that day; as
the French are faid to have owed the
mildnefs of their defpotifm to the SWEET
BLOOD of the Bourbons.

In fuch a fituation of affairs, if I
thought with Tully, which I certainly
do not, the *poffe fi velit* * a fufficient
caufe for recurring to refiftance and revolution in point of right, I fhould confider
fuch a conjuncture in point of expediency

---

* Quæ caufa juftior eft bella gerandi, quam fervitutis
depulfio? in qua etiamfi non fit moleftus dominus, tamen
eft mifenimum poffe fi velit.

as

as of all others the moſt unpropitious to
any ſtrong effort in favour of liberty. The
people as I have obſerved before, muſt feel
the actual preſſure of the evil and feel it
pretty ſtrongly too before they can be
made to move. They will not hazard
preſent good for contingent advantage;
and in this I think their groſs good ſenſe
directs them perfectly well; for premature reſiſtance inſtead of ſerving the
cauſe of liberty, has generally ended in
moſt effectually playing the game into the
hands of power; it furniſhes the very de-
ſired pretext, and turns glorious and honourable contention into treaſon and rebellion. In ſuch order of things, action
being neither neceſſary nor expedient, I
would endeavour to provide for the future by turning the thoughts and attention

tion of men to the paſt; the GLORIOUS REVOLUTION ſhould be perpetually recalled to their remembrance, and the immortal decree of the Convention Parliament continually impreſſed upon their minds as the great fundamental law of the conſtitution. If this is the object of the Revolution Society, and I am ſure I do not know that it is not, I ſhould be proud to ſee my humble name upon its rolls. To the Revolution this nation owes a hundred years of liberty and proſperity, and if we do not " forget the Lord which " brought us forth out of the land of " Ægypt from the houſe of bondage" it may prolong the bleſſing to an hundred more. Let us then " teach it diligently " to our children, let us talk of it when " we ſit in our houſes, and when we " walk

" walk by the way; when we lie down
" and when we rife up; let us bind it
" for a fign upon our hands and as a
" frontlet between our eyes; let us write
" it upon the pofts of our houfe and on
" our gates." To Kings and Minifters
too it furnifhed a moft admirable pre-
ventative leffon. Inftead of endeavouring to prolong their Afiatic dream with
foft lullabies to the tune of divine right
and paffive obedience, I would find
them where they lay afleep and hollow
in their ear REVOLUTION. Revolution
fhould refound through the palaces of
Kings and the levee-rooms of Minifters.
Far from endeavouring to hide—

" This word of fear,
" Unpleafing to a royal ear,"

in the tawdry rags of fophiftry, I would
                                    prefent

prefent it to them in large and legible characters, that he that runneth might read. I would write it upon the wall at the feaft of Balfhazzar; I would force them to look up to it, like the " bow in " the cloud, as the token of a covenant " for perpetual generations."

We will if you pleafe carry on the fiction a little farther; we will figure to ourfelves one of our future Kings in the conftant habit of receiving unlimited obedience from men, cafting a jealous eye towards the ftubborn unpliancy of the laws. He feels his power, and his mind hefitates. In this ftate of doubt he feeks for counfel. An honeft whig-privy-councillor on that day might I think exprefs himfelf in terms fomething like the following: Sire, I fhould ill repay the con-

fidence

fidence with which your Majefty is pleafed to honour me if I did not give you
my opinion with truth and fincerity. If
your Majefty will deign to confider your
people not as your private property but as a
truft committed to your charge, your good
fenfe and the goodnefs of your heart will I
think eafily lead you to perceive that you
can have no claim to take away or abridge
any of their rights or to alter any of their
fundamental laws; your Majefty knows
that the good of the people is the end,
the fupreme law, the only true foundation of all government. In the excellent
conftitution of this kingdom it has been
carefully provided to feparate the *execu-*
tive from the *legiflative*, becaufe whenever
thefe two powers came to be held by the
fame hands either directly or indirectly

P   laws

laws will be made not for the advantage or fecurity of the public, but for the eafe or fafety or aggrandifement of the governing power. Your Majefty poffeffes in right of your Crown the whole of the executive power over your realms in its utmoft extent, and as much of the legiflative only as is neceffary for the prefervation of the rights of your Crown. For this purpofe you are entrufted with a negative voice upon all new laws, but with no power to alter or originate laws becaufe every law being a renunciation of fome portion of natural liberty to obtain fome advantage at leaft equivalent to what is given up, this fort of exchange can only be made by the perfons to whom the property belongs; by the nation or its agents and reprefentatives. Your Majefty

will

will I am fure perceive that it is the pofitive and immediate duty of thefe agents
to take the utmoft care of the interefts
of their employers, and efpecially to fee
that in no cafe whatfoever more liberty is
given up than is fairly purchafed by the
protection or other advantages obtained in
exchange. In the common proceedings
of life an agent who fhould act otherwife
would incur that fort of infamy which
renders a man unfit for the fociety of
people of character and honour, and this
infamy would extend alfo to any perfons
of what rank foever who fhould tamper
with thefe agents, to endeavour to feduce
them by perfonal influence or bribes or
threats to give up the rights and properties of their principals upon terms of un-
equal exchange or for the exprefs pur-

pofes

pofes of being ufed to their detriment or
annoyance. I will therefore venture humbly to ftate to your Majefty that your rights
are ftrictly confined to the exercife of the
executive power and to the fimple nega-
tion on all propofed laws; and that you
have no claim in juftice or reafon either
by yourfelf or your Minifters to govern
and direct the legiflation.

Having with great humility ftated to
your Majefty what I take to be the *rights*
of a King of Great Britain, I will venture
to affert that your *interefts* exactly coincide
with them. To the fuperior excellence
of the government this country is in-
debted for its fuperior rank among the
nations far above its proportion of numbers or extent. Men are encouraged to
every ufeful exertion by the certainty of
enjoying

enjoying the fruits of their induſtry or
ingenuity. The arts, the commerce, the
riches, the proſperity of your Majeſty's
people are owing to the ſecurity of their
perſons and properties under a free conſtitution. Remove this ſecurity and ta-
lents and induſtry will inſtantly ſeek it
where it is elſewhere to be found.
Inſtead of the Monarch of a great and
powerful nation confident againſt a world
in arms, holding in your hand the balance
among the powers of the world, you would
ſink into the petty prince of a petty people,
the dependant of ſome great ſtate or the
confederate of a ſmall one; ſo that your
Majeſty's *greatneſs* is owing to the influence of theſe very laws now in queſtion
before us. Nor is the *happineſs* of your
Majeſty leſs concerned in the preſervation

of

of the conftitution than your greatnefs. You ftand in a fituation perhaps unmatched in the relative pofitions of men. You have unlimited authority to do good and none to do harm ; every faculty to create reverence and love and no power to excite envy or anger ; with lefs effort than is neceffary to fill the loweft offices of life you are fecure of a perpetual empire over the hearts of a naturally loyal and generous people. After the *right* and *expediency* we come to confider the point of *fact*; whether your Majefty could with fafety to your Crown overturn the fundamental laws of the conftitution, and I am firmly of opinion that you could not. Though the people are luxurious and profligate and apparently indifferent to public meafures, if your Majefty's Minifters

were

2

were to put forth their hands and touch any of thofe laws which the people have been ufed to confider as the *palladia* of their liberties, another order of things would prefently take place. " It would " operate as a call upon the nation." The people would roufe from their lethargy; men would affociate and combine and con-vene; the found of " To your tents, O If-" rael !" would be propagated in low mur-murs from the Hebrides to the Land's End. Your Majefty well knows what paffed in 1688, and there is no reafon in the world to believe that the fame caufe would not again produce the fame effect. The re-fiftance of the people would indeed be much more eafy and direct than it was at that time, becaufe a grand precedent has been eftablifhed; there is now a leading

cafe

cafe in point; they have tracks and guide-
pofts and land-marks which they had not
before; befides the more recent examples
of America and France and even Ireland
before their eyes. Thefe, Sire, are, the
opinions of a plain man fincerely attached
to your Majefty's perfon and government,
but holding a ftill ftronger bond of attachment to the laws and conftitution of my
country.

The Tories of that day would not fail
to take the oppofite ground. They would
obferve that there is all the difference in
the world between obtaining a repeal of
thefe fundamental laws by the good-will
and confent of Parliament and endeavouring to carry on government without the
aid of Parliament. That liberty-may be
a fine thing but that politenefs and gallantry

lantry and loyalty are infinitely finer.
That the Revolution about which a few
factious republicans made fuch a rout
went much more upon the preſervation of
the Proteſtant hierarchy of the church of
England and the privileges of Parliament
than upon any nonſenſical abſtract notions
of the *rights of the people*. That if the nation did upon that occaſion *feem* to elect
a King, they well knew that they were
doing what they had no right to do, they
did it as if they were aſhamed of it, keeping it from the eye with a fort of pick-
pocket addreſs, and the moment it was
over renouncing any fuch right in future
for ever ; that provided the eccleſiaſtical
and civil eſtabliſhments are preſerved, and
above all provided the *loaves* and *fiſhes* can
continue to be diſtributed ſo that the

Q   " multitude

" multitude may eat and be filled" all will be well; that men are tired of altercation and wifh only for enjoyment; that indeed what has been done in America and France has made the people almoft fick of the very name of liberty.

Before I conclude let me proteft againft being mifunderftood. I am no abettor of faction. You, Sir, cannot love peace and order and fubordination and tranquillity more than I do. Anarchy and confufion and civil difcord cannot be more your abhorrence than they are mine *. I only infift that we have *conftitutional rights* and *fundamental laws,* all attacks upon which the nation has as much right to

* Nec privatos focos, nec publicas leges, nec libertatis jura cura habere poteft, quem difcordia, quem cædes civium, quem bellum civile delectat; eumque ex numero hominum ejeciendum, ex finibus humanæ naturæ exterminandum puto.   Cic.

refift as every individual has to repel the force of a highwayman; refiftance is no more rebellion in one cafe than killing is murder in the other. Thefe are extreme cafes and require extreme remedies.—Why, Sir, do you call upon us to moot points on thefe delicate and dangerous topics? The very confideration of them is omenous; it tends to fill the mind with vain fears and falfe alarms. God avert them from thefe kingdoms! with very little reliance on human wifdom and virtue we may hope and truft that Government will ever be as backward to provoke violence as the people ought to be to recur to it. No man in the world would hear what you fo emphatically term "'a call of the nation *" with more dread and horrour than I fhould

* Letter to Meffrs. Farr and Harris, p. 16.

do. But ftill I hope I fhould obey that call if the occafion really demanded it. I am fure if I did not I muft for ever after live a coward in mine own efteem.

I was born and nurtered in the old-fafhioned defpifed principles of Whig-gifm, and in thefe principles I fhall certainly die. They are the prejudices of my infancy confirmed by the reafon of my riper age. One of the fundamental articles of the fymbol of political faith in which I received my firft rudiments of inftruction is, that the prefent Royal Family were *called by the nation* to the throne of thefe kingdoms to defend and fupport our religion and liberties and laws ; that they have entered into a *folemn contract* to this effect, and *receive the allegiance* of the people upon *thefe terms* and *thefe terms* only.

only. In the Declaration of Rights the
" people" " *claim demand* and *infift* upon"
" all and fingular the premifes as their
" *undoubted rights* and liberties." In the
Bill of Rights " all and fingular the *rights*
" and *liberties afferted* and *claimed* in the
" faid Declaration are recognized to be
" the true, antient and *indubitable rights*
" *of the people.*" In the Act of Settlement
limiting the crown to the prefent Royal
Family, they are declared to be " the
" *birthright* of the people of England."
Thefe were the doctrines by which I was
early taught a loyal attachment to the il-
luftrious Houfe of Hanover. Thefe were
the doctrines of the Courts of George the
Firft and George the Second. They were
proud to be told that they reigned by the
free choice of a free people. Hereditary
right

right and unlimited fubmiffion were then the watch-words of faction and rebellion. Thefe, Sir, are the doctrines for which I contend becaufe I believe them to be per-fectly conftitutional. I go no farther. I fufpect I was tempted to anfwer your letter merely upon account of that paffage where you feem to fay that the nation abdicated and renounced at the Revolution the right of *claiming demanding* and *infifting* upon their *undoubted rights* and *liberties,* the *birthright* of the *people of England* by any future interruption of the fucceffion.

I will now take my leave. It is high time to put an end to this defultory letter already I fear much too long. I will finifh as I began with the moft fincere affurances of refpect and efteem. I think I have feen it fomewhere mentioned that you have

have been or are to be prefented with ho-
nary degrees in our univerfities; and that
your work is admired and praifed by the
higheft perfonages. I fincerely hope fomething more folid will follow. Honours
cannot be placed on a more deferving head
or truft committed into purer hands.   I
am perfuaded that there is not a man in
the nation whofe elevation would be received with lefs envy or more univerfal
approbation.   To give a dignified repofe
to the evening of a life like yours would
equally honour the receiving and the con-
ferring hand.

My clients have nothing of this fort to
difpofe of; they have nothing to give but
barren applaufe; and they commonly beftow that with fuch incapacity of judgment that a wife man will not be much
flattered with the acquifition. There is

indeed another fort of applaufe of which
I confefs myfelf more ambitious, an applaufe which the world can neither give
nor take away, and which cannot be bought
with ftarts of patriotifm or hypocritical
grimace; an applaufe, Sir, of which I am
perfuaded no man knows the value better
than you do, and which will not fail to
gild your fetting day with more cheering
rays than ever emanated from the fmiles
of Minifters or Kings, I mean the applaufe
of our own confciences.—Adieu then,
good Sir—accept my fincere falutations,
and the regard and confideration with
which I am

Your faithful and moft humble fervant,

BROOKE BOOTHBY.

Afhberne Hall,
Dec. 27, 1790.

E R R A T A.

Page 3, l. 4, for *bye*, read *by*.
— 3, l. 13, for *such*, read *much*.
— 13, note, for *proti* read *proh*.
— 24, l. 8, for *being*, read *beings?*
— 31, l. 7, for *contripetal*, read *centripetal*.
— 39, l. 1, for *imprimateurs*, read *imprimaturs*.
— 40, l. 14, for *continues*, read *continue*.
— 42, l. 2, for *drawn*, read *driven*.
— 43, l. 7, for *convertable*, read *convertible*.
— 46, l. 2, before *reason*, add *own*.
— 48, l. 5, before *Hierarchy*, add *A*.
— 56, l. the last, for *loose*, read *looser*.
— 68, l. 14, for *ex-bishops*, read *exbishop*.
— 81, l. 14, for *natis*, read *pati*.
— 99, l. 11, for *aspectantis*, read *aspectantes*.
— 103, l. 7, for *furnished*, read *furnishes*.
— 104, l. 17, for *on*, read *of*,
— 105, l. 18, for *came*, read *come*.
— 115, l. 8, for *omenous*, read *ominous*
— 116, l. 5, for *nurtered*, read *nurtured*.